snow
music

snow music

BY Lynne Rae Perkins

SCHOLASTIC INC.

New York   Toronto   London   Auckland   Sydney
Mexico City   New Delhi   Hong Kong   Buenos Aires

Everyone whisper:

peth peth

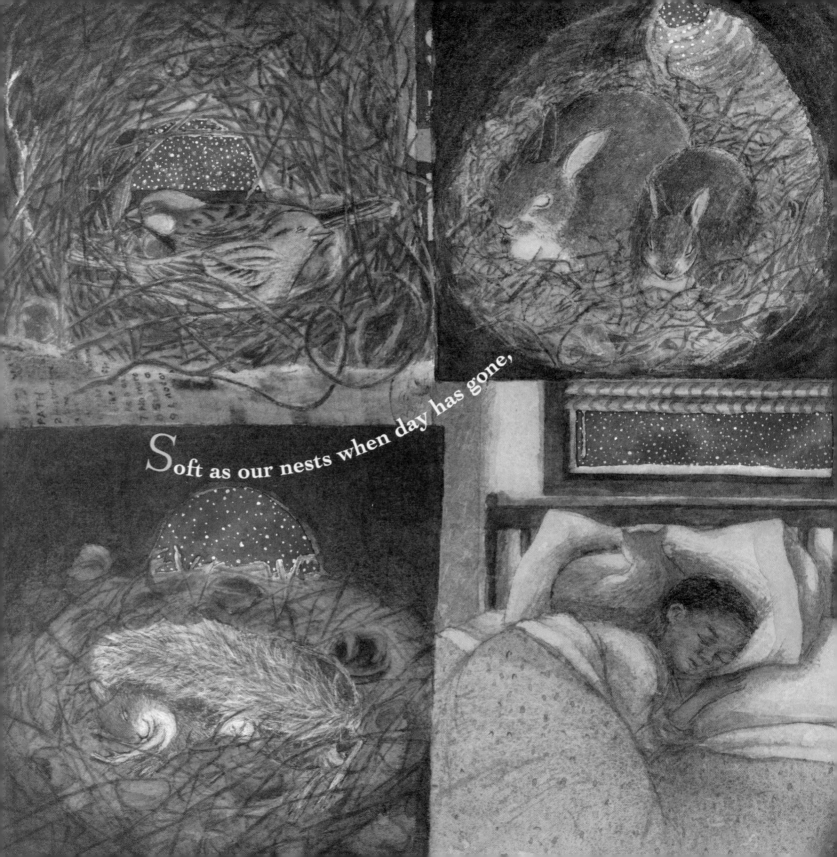

Soft as our nests when day has gone,

Snow came singing a silent song.

Night

was here,

but she

left at

dawn.

Shhhhhhhhh

Oops.

What is the sound of one bird hopping?

Does the deer

feel the cold   of the snow

in her hoofs?

hop hop hop hop hop

I think—

I think

I left it—

I think

I left it

here—

somewhere . . .

I think.

wait—

No,

it here . . .

I left

I know

I think I—

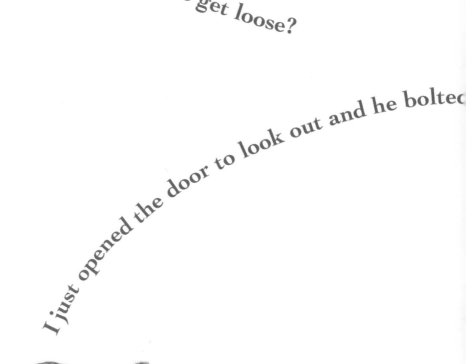

No, did he get loose?

I just opened the door to look out and he bolted

You say something like,
Hi.

I say something like,
Hi.
Have you seen my dog?

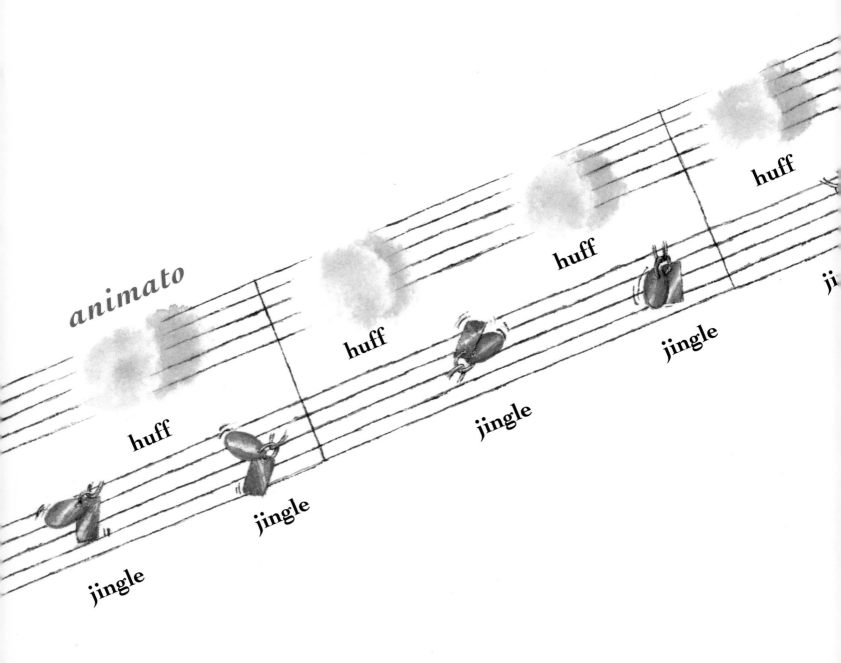

A CAR WENT BY

poot poot poot poot poot poot poot poot poot poot . . .

Someone inside was drawing in the frost on the window.

plop

We could hear its radio playing. (Cover your mouth with your hand and sing a song from the radio.)

TRUCK SONG

(LOUD)

Truck noise:

The scraping

of the plow,

the tires.

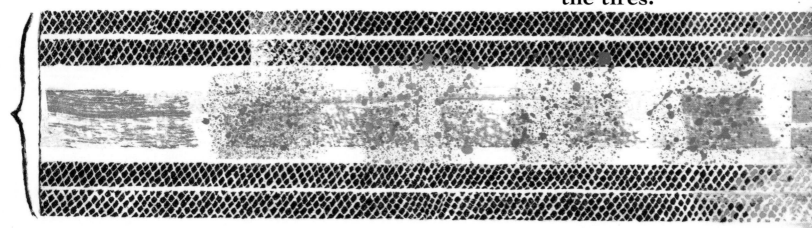

Bursts of sand and salt hit the road.

Did you
find him?
No.
No.

All of us looking for something to eat.
The sun came looking for something to heat.

It found the snow, and the deer's cold feet.

There he is!
I see him!

K-tk.

Good boy.

Why are you
saying he's good?

So he'll like
coming home.

Click.

Quick, and as
quiet as a
bunny on a
road. Swift,
and as silent
as the shadow
of a crow.

Clouds
crept in
and started
to snow.

Everyone whisper:

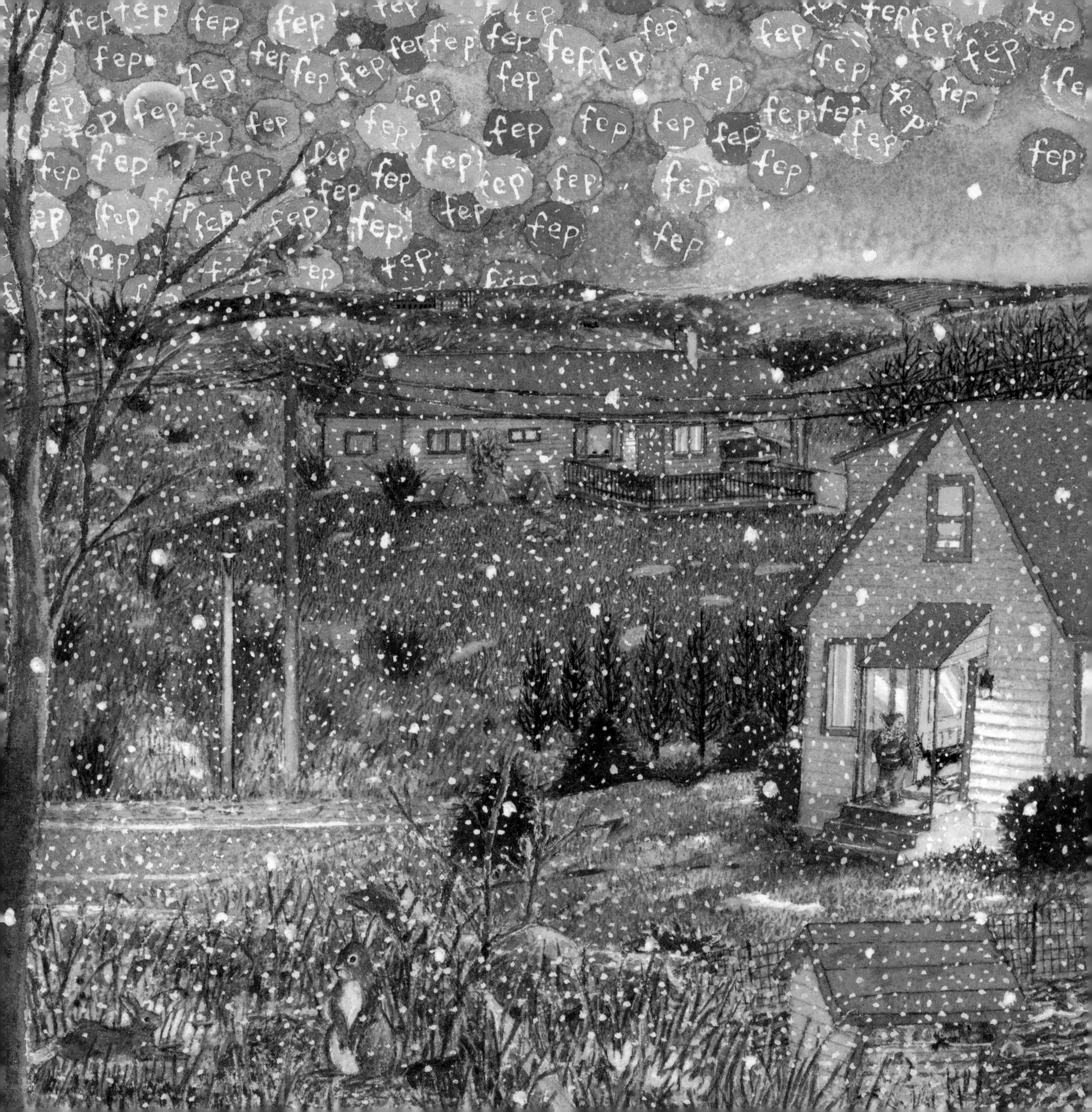
fep
fep
fep

For Bill and Lucky,
the great rogues

ISBN 0-439-67773-4

12 11 10 9 8 7 6 5 4 3 2 1   4 5 6 7 8 9/0

Printed in the U.S.A.   40

First Scholastic printing, November 2004

Pen and ink and watercolor paints were used to prepare the full-color art.
The text type is 20-point Cochin Bold.